HAUNTED STATES
of
AMERICA

HAUNT
— and —
SEEK

Book design by Sarah Taplin
Cover illustration by Maggie Ivy
Interior illustrations by Eszter Szépvölgyi

Published in the United States by Jolly Fish Press, an imprint of North Star Editions, Inc.

First Edition
First Printing, 2020

This is a work of fiction. Names, characters, places, and incidents are either the product of the author's imagination or are used fictitiously, and any resemblance to actual persons living or dead, business establishments, events, or locales is entirely coincidental.

Library of Congress Cataloging-in-Publication Data
Names: Troupe, Thomas Kingsley, author.
Title: Haunt and seek / Thomas Kingsley Troupe.
Description: First Edition. | Mendota Heights, Minnesota : Jolly Fish
    Press, 2021. | Series: Haunted States of America | Audience: Grades 4-6.
    | Summary: "Ben Tajima spots a ghostly boy all over town during a visit
    with his grandparents to Chicago, Illinois"— Provided by publisher.
Identifiers: LCCN 2020004422 (print) | LCCN 2020004423 (ebook) | ISBN
    9781631634765 (paperback) | ISBN 9781631634758 (hardcover) | ISBN
    9781631634772 (ebook)
Subjects: CYAC: Ghosts—Fiction. | Grandparents—Fiction. | Chicago
    (Ill.)—Fiction.
Classification: LCC PZ7.T7538 Hau 2021 (print) | LCC PZ7.T7538 (ebook) |
    DDC [Fic]—dc23
LC record available at https://lccn.loc.gov/2020004422
LC ebook record available at https://lccn.loc.gov/2020004423

Jolly Fish Press
North Star Editions, Inc.
2297 Waters Drive
Mendota Heights, MN 55120
www.jollyfishpress.com

Printed in the United States of America

HAUNTED STATES
of
AMERICA

HAUNT
— and —
SEEK

THOMAS KINGSLEY TROUPE

JOLLY
FiSH
PRESS

Mendota Heights, Minnesota

CHAPTER 1

WINDY CITY

Ben Tajima couldn't believe people sometimes. About halfway through their five-and a half-hour bus ride from Columbus, Ohio, to Chicago, Illinois, he saw something he didn't expect.

The middle-aged guy across the aisle from him had taken his shoes and socks off. It was bad enough seeing the man's grungy bare feet and toenails. Even worse? They could have used a trim maybe a month or two ago. Even worse than that? He was picking the lint from between his toes and dropping what he found on the ground.

"Gross," Lola, his younger sister, said aloud.

She was looking over at the man from the seat next to Ben. Her voice was loud enough for the man to look up from his work. As the man started to turn his head, Ben elbowed Lola, then pretended to be engrossed in his book again.

"What?" Lola whispered.

Ben leaned forward to cut off her view of the man.

His heart thumped in his chest. He didn't know if the guy was staring at them with his bare feet hanging out or not, but it sure felt like it.

He. Can. Hear. You, Ben mouthed to Lola, his eyes burning into hers.

"Well, it's disgusting," Lola said, back at normal volume.

"Please just watch your videos," Ben said.

"Please don't act like you're the boss of me," Lola replied, mocking her older brother.

Ben groaned. It was his parents' idea to send the two

of them to Chicago to visit their grandparents. Their grandparents had moved there a few months ago. But their parents didn't want to pay for an expensive plane ticket or drive them back and forth themselves, so they had decided to send them on a bus. Seeing that Ben was almost fifteen years old and Lola was pretty much thirteen, they were old enough to make the trip themselves.

It'll be a good experience for you, Dad had said. *Besides, Grandma and Grandpa will pick you up.*

Seemed simple enough, but no one took into account how difficult Lola could be sometimes. Where Ben was quiet and kept to himself, Lola didn't really care what anyone else thought. Being stuck in a metal tube on wheels for over five hours with his little sister wasn't his idea of a good time. Ben was, thankfully, looking forward to seeing his grandparents.

When he felt the coast was clear, Ben looked over to see the man across the aisle had replaced his socks and shoes and was scrolling through something on his phone. He wondered if the man's phone smelled like feet.

The last few hours of the bus ride were fine. Lola only had to get up two more times to use the restroom, and each time she complained about how bumpy it was and how much it stank in there. As they got closer to the city, a baby began to cry.

I'm ready to get off this bus too, kid, Ben thought.

After navigating the inner-city traffic, the bus pulled into the Race Dog bus transit terminal. It was a flat one-level building with eight bays for other buses to pull into. Once the bus came to a stop and the air brakes hissed, the passengers stood up. Ben heard people groan as they got to their feet. Sitting still for five-plus hours was a long time, and he too was happy to be able to stand and stretch his legs.

Carrying their small backpacks, Ben and Lola stepped off the Race Dog bus and headed toward the terminal. Above the door was a blue metal sign with the bus company's running-dog logo on it. Below the silver racing pooch, it said: WELCOME TO CHICAGO, IL.

"So are Grandma and Grandpa supposed to meet us out here, or . . . ," Lola began, looking around.

"They're probably inside," Ben replied.

He paused at the door for a moment to listen. The city was loud and alive with the sounds of traffic roaring along the streets and overhead on a freeway overpass.

As they walked inside, they saw rows of benches where people were waiting for their departing buses or the arrival of friends and family. It, like the rest of the city, was busy and seemingly hectic for a Thursday afternoon.

"I don't see them," Lola said, popping her earbuds out for the first time since their trip began. "Are we sure we're at the right station?"

Ben scanned the crowd. There was a family of five huddled in front of a vending machine, their suitcases piled around them. A line of about twelve people stood at the ticket counters. Moving quickly through the crowd and heading their way were two older people. When they made eye contact with Ben, they lifted up a small hand-made sign. On it were a series of Japanese characters.

"Yeah, we're at the right station," Ben said, smiling at his grandparents and waving.

After the hugs Grandma showed them the sign she was holding again.

"Did you like the sign?" she asked.

"Yeah," Ben said, knowing what was coming next. "It was really great."

Grandma narrowed her eyes and pointed. "You don't know what it says."

He stared at the sign, trying to make sense of the Japanese characters she'd written out.

It was no use. He and Lola were supposed to practice and learn his culture's language, but it was daunting for someone who'd grown up speaking English in suburban Ohio.

"No," Ben admitted. "I don't. Sorry."

Grandma pointed out the characters and slowly said each word, as if that would help him instantly learn Japanese.

"Welcome to the Windy City," she said.

"Oh, okay," Ben said, smiling. "Very nice."

He liked that his grandparents were proud of their family's culture, even if Grandma and Grandpa hadn't been to Japan since they were in their thirties.

"We'll work on that," Grandma said. She patted Ben's arm a few times as if to tell him it would be all right. Her smile was enough to make him smile right back at her.

"Are we ready to go?" Grandpa asked.

Ben and Lola gathered their bags and followed their grandparents out of the station.

"Seriously?" Lola asked. "Another bus? We just got off one!"

After a short wait at the bus stop, Ben, Lola, and their grandparents were riding the bus through the streets of Chicago. Ben took a window seat and looked at all of the buildings they passed by. Some of them seemed three times as tall as the ones in their downtown back home. His grandpa caught him looking at the enormous skyscraper that towered over the rest of the city.

"Sears Tower," Grandpa said, leaning close to the window to look up as high as he could.

"It's Willis Tower now," Grandma corrected. "Second tallest building in North America," she added.

"Really?" Ben said, looking at it. It was shaped as if it were a cluster of buildings smashed together. It really did seem to go up forever.

"Yes," Grandpa said, almost proudly, as if he'd helped build it. "They have a glass box you can stand in up there. On the one hundred and third floor, almost one thousand four hundred feet up. You can look down and see the city below you and can see across the city for miles and miles."

"No way," Lola said. "We have to do that."

Ben wasn't too crazy about the idea.

"It's a little bit scary," Grandma admitted. "You can actually feel the building sway when you're up there."

"The building sways?" Ben asked. "As in like it could snap in half and fall over?"

"Oh, sure," Lola said. "From all the wind, being the Windy City and all that."

Grandpa laughed and adjusted his Cubs hat, shaking his head.

"Oh no, no, Lola," he said. "It would never snap. That's not possible."

After seeing a few more Chicago landmarks on their way to their grandparents' new home, the Tajimas arrived at the 100 block of West Wacker Drive.

Ben looked up at the building his grandparents now called home. It was completely different from what he'd expected. Their house in Ohio had been small and old and cozy. The metal-and-glass tower in front of him . . . was not.

"You guys seriously live here?" Ben asked. Since when did his grandparents become so . . . hip? Didn't most older people like the peace and quiet of a suburban neighborhood?

Downtown Chicago definitely was not quiet.

"Yes," Grandpa said, smiling so much that his face was even more wrinkly than normal. "It has great views, and we're less than thirty minutes from Wrigley Field. It's perfect for your grandma and me."

"We love it here." Grandma nodded in agreement.

Grandpa turned Ben around so that he could show him the river right across the street. He explained that the river ran right through the city and was connected to Lake Michigan, one of the Great Lakes.

"That's pretty cool," Lola said. "Do people fish in this river?"

Grandma laughed. "Not many," she said. "There are fish in there, but they're probably not good for eating. The river is a little polluted, being here in the city."

"So no swimming," Lola said. "Got it."

"You can swim inside," Grandpa said, leading them

13

to their building. "Come, come. Let us show you our new place!"

———————

To put it simply, Ben's grandparents' new home was amazing. There was a small convenience store in the lobby so they never had to go too far if they ran out of milk or needed some chips. There was a huge workout room with treadmills and other exercise machines that looked out into the city. Near that was the swimming pool, which seemed even bigger than the one at their school back home. The place seemed brand new and fancy, and Ben couldn't help but think his grandparents didn't really fit in there.

Even so, they seemed happy, and that was all that mattered.

When they finally got to their actual apartment, Ben and Lola were amazed at the view they had on the twenty-second floor. They could see more of the impressive buildings of downtown Chicago, the river, and even a little hint of Lake Michigan itself. It made Ben a little dizzy just looking out the window.

Their grandparents showed them the rest of the apartment, and Ben was relieved to see that he and his sister weren't going to have to share rooms. They each had their own space and a bathroom to share.

"This place is pretty incredible," Lola said, walking through the living room. She stopped to admire the fish they had in a large tank. "Are these koi fish?"

Grandpa nodded as he tried to find the Cubs game on his large TV. Ben knew one of the biggest reasons his grandparents had wanted to move to Chicago was to be able to see as many baseball games as possible. Even living in Ohio, they didn't care for the Cleveland Indians or the Cincinnati Reds.

It was always the Chicago Cubs for some reason.

"We're going to take you to the game on Saturday," Grandpa said. "Give you a big taste of why we love this city."

"Okay, cool," Ben said.

He wasn't a huge fan of baseball but didn't have any problem taking in a game. He was sort of wondering what else they'd do during their visit, and it sounded like some of their Saturday was all set.

As Ben set his bag down in his room for the weekend, he saw a small card lying on his bed. There were Japanese characters carefully printed on the front, along with a few small red hearts.

I have no idea what that says, Ben thought.

He picked up the card and saw that the English translation was written inside:

We're glad you're here.

Love, Grandma and Grandpa

CHAPTER 2

TINY TREASURE

After letting Ben and Lola settle into their rooms a bit, Grandpa told everyone to get their shoes on.

"Where are we going?" Lola asked as she headed into the kitchen. She pulled one of her earbuds out to divide her attention between her phone and her grandparents.

"It's time for a taste of Chicago," Grandpa said, pulling his Cubs cap over his mostly bald head. "We're going to get some deep dish pizza at Big Lorenzo's."

"Deep dish?" Ben asked. "Like how deep are we talking about?"

"Oh," Grandpa said, holding his pointer finger and thumb apart, "Three to four inches, tops."

Ben watched as his grandfather helped his grandmother put on a windbreaker. She zipped it up and slung a small purse over her shoulder. Even though they were just heading out to eat somewhere, it almost looked like they were gearing up for a great adventure.

"Wallet, keys, kids," Grandpa said as he patted his

pockets, then pointed at Ben and Lola. "We're ready to go."

The four of them took the elevator down to the main floor and walked through the fancy lobby. It was still fairly light outside, one of the things Ben liked best about summer.

Not that he was scared of the dark or anything. He was a teenager, after all.

The walk to Big Lorenzo's was short and didn't even require them taking a bus, something Lola was happy about. They found a table in the crowded restaurant after a short wait and ordered their food and drinks. They drank three sodas each while they waited for their pizza.

Lola leaned over to Ben. "No way would Mom and Dad let us get refills," she whispered.

Grandma shrugged. "Grandparents are supposed to spoil their grandchildren," she said. "Just be sure to brush those teeth really well. You mom would be displeased if we sent you home with rotten teeth."

Ben covered his teeth with his lips and pretended that all of them had fallen out. "Mom? Dad?" he said. "Sorry. We had too many sugary drinks."

The four of them laughed, and as they waited for

their food, they caught up on everything they'd been up to over the summer. At one point Lola looked at the time on her phone.

"Seriously," she said. "How long does it take to cook a pizza?"

"Ah," Grandpa said. "Perfection takes time. And the pizzas here?"

"Perfection?" Ben offered.

Grandpa nodded and gave him a thumbs-up.

At long last the pizza came. Ben would go on to brag to his friends back in Columbus that he'd had the most insanely delicious pizza he'd ever sunk his teeth into. It was thick with sauce and gooey with cheese and was every bit worth the wait. Even Lola couldn't argue.

The sun was setting by the time they walked back to their grandparents' apartment. They walked along the sidewalk near the river and watched as a tour boat slowly motored along the water, the guide onboard pointing out some of the city's landmarks as they drifted by.

"We should do that," Lola said. "That looks like fun."

"A little history wrapped up in a boat ride," Grandma said. "Maybe we can fit that into our plans."

As the four of them watched the boat glide by, something along the sidewalk caught Ben's attention. He headed toward a stone bench set along the walkway. There was something kind of shiny wedged into a small patch of mud just underneath the bench's legs. Thinking it was a coin at first, he squatted to get a closer look.

He reached down to pick it up and saw that it wasn't a coin after all, but something a bit bigger and not nearly as flat. With a gentle tug, he freed the object from the mud and saw that it was a small metal boat. The little boat felt cool to the touch, likely from the wet soil it had been wedged into.

"Hey, Benji," Lola said. "You picking up garbage again?"

"Not exactly," Ben said, turning the half-mud-caked boat in his hand. "But do I need to remind you about the time I found fifty bucks on the ground?"

"Yeah, yeah," Lola said. "A once-in-a-lifetime jackpot. Big deal. What is that thing?"

Ben held it up and brushed a little more of the mud away.

Lola nodded. "Okay, that is pretty cool," she admitted.

Thinking it might be an antique trinket of some sort, Ben tucked the small boat into the pocket of his shorts. They headed away from the river toward the apartment building across the street.

"So how long do we have to wait to swim?" Lola called from her bedroom around twenty minutes later.

Ben groaned from his own room as he changed into his swimsuit.

"You don't have to wait after eating," Ben shouted back. "We've had this conversation before. Swimming after eating doesn't affect your stomach."

"Well, excuse me for not wanting my stomach to get

tied up in a knot and make me drown," Lola snapped. "I don't want to get cramps."

Trying to keep his room here at least a little tidier than his own room back home, Ben set his shorts on the bed. As he did, he saw a glint just before he heard the sound of something metallic hitting the wood floor.

Ben crouched near the bed to see what it was but couldn't find it. Instead, he saw a small piece of dirt on the floor and realized what it must have been.

The little boat!

He got down on all fours and peered under the bed to see if he could find it. There, lying on its side, was the small, dirty metal boat he'd found outside. Ben grabbed it and stood up to look at it. There were still bits of dirt and mud wedged into the details of the tiny ship. The thing looked old and pretty beat up for something made of metal.

Maybe it's an antique? Ben thought, turning it over in his hand. He didn't know much about the value of old things but had seen plenty of shows where people got them appraised by experts. One guy had an old comic book that was worth almost ten thousand dollars.

With dollar signs in his eyes, Ben brought the little boat into the bathroom with him. He turned on the faucet and ran it under the water, knocking the remaining dirt and mud out of the boat's nooks and crannies. In a matter of seconds, the toy boat was as clean as it could be.

Ben set the boat on the hand towel on the vanity to let it dry.

"Ben!" Lola shouted from the hallway. "Are you about ready to go?"

"Coming," Ben said, drying off his hands. He opened the door, and she threw his towel at him. He flinched and exhaled once to show his annoyance.

"Hey," Lola said as they walked out into the living room. "You guys aren't going to swim with us?"

Grandpa shook his head. "Oh, no. Too late for us to swim tonight."

Ben thought about that. *There's a good and a bad time to swim?* He knew that if they had a swimming pool at their house back home, he'd be swimming around the clock.

"But we'll come along and watch," Grandma said. "Watch the two of you splash around for a bit."

The four of them rode the elevator to the second floor, then walked down the hallway, past the workout room, and toward a set of double doors. Even from thirty feet away, Ben could smell the chlorine in the water.

They opened the doors, and Lola startled the rest of the group by cheering.

"Yes!" she shouted. "We get the pool to ourselves!"

Ben looked to see she was right. There wasn't another soul in the swimming pool or even the nearby hot tub. The chairs arranged around the tables were empty, with no one anywhere else in sight.

Grandma and Grandpa found some chairs near the edge of the pool and sat down with their towels as Lola wasted no time in jumping from the edge and into the nine-foot deep end. She sprang back up through the surface and wiped her hair from her face.

"Let's go, Ben!" she shouted. "The water is amazing."

Ben walked to the edge, careful not to slip.

Dipping his foot into the water, Ben confirmed that his sister was right. The water really was perfect. He stepped off the edge and slipped in, plugging his nose before his face hit. His entire body was enveloped in the water, and he felt the rush as he dipped below the surface. When his feet touched the bottom, he sprang back up.

"Oh, nice," Ben said, wiping the water from his eyes.

He thought they could easily spend the entire weekend in the pool and he wouldn't be too upset.

As Lola climbed back out over and over to perfect her cannonball, Ben swam beneath the surface, trying to see if he could swim from one side of the pool to the other without coming up for air. He came close, rising to the surface a few feet from the edge. When he looked back at his grandparents, he could see them watching and giving approving nods.

"Almost, Benji!" Grandma shouted.

Not wanting to admit defeat, Ben tried again. He grasped the edge of the pool and turned himself around. Sucking in a huge lungful of air, he dove beneath the surface of the water and swam.

Somewhere around the halfway point to the other side, Ben opened his eyes. The chlorinated water stung a bit, but he wanted to see where he was going and how close he was to his goal. A small dark shape moved to his right, and he turned.

It looked like someone was standing at the bottom of the pool.

Lola! Ben thought, and kept swimming. He glanced again to see what she was doing, but it was difficult to

see. Feeling his air running low, he kicked ahead until his fingers touched the other side of the pool.

He burst through the surface and looked up to see his sister and grandparents watching him from the pool deck.

Grandma and Grandpa clapped. Lola smirked.

"Show off," she said.

Ben ignored her comment and looked up at her.

"How did you get out of the water so quick?" he asked.

"Ummm . . . ," she began, looking at him like he was losing it. "I climbed out?"

Ben looked back at the spot where he'd seen the figure, only to discover that there was no one there. He turned and scanned the rest of the pool, wondering if some other people had joined them while he was doing his side-to-side swim challenge.

Ben and his family were still the only ones in the pool area.

"Very funny," he said. "You must've climbed out and run back over here."

"What are you talking about?" Lola asked. She looked to her grandparents as if seeking their support.

Ben rubbed his eyes, which still stung from the

chlorine. He went back underwater and peered around the pool, looking to figure out what it was he might've seen. There was nothing.

He surfaced again, shaking his head.

"I saw something down there," Ben insisted.

Lola lowered her eyebrows and then raised one, puzzled.

"Well, it wasn't me," she said slowly.

Ben looked to his grandparents, who were now standing up and looking to the spot in the deep end their grandson was pointing to.

"Did you see anything?" Ben asked. "Right over there?"

Both of them looked as confused as Ben felt.

"It's just been you and Lola swimming," Grandpa insisted. "No one else."

Even though the pool was heated just slightly, a cold chill ran down Ben's spine. When he grasped the ladder to pull himself out of the pool, he could see the telltale goose bumps on his arms. He wasn't cold, but something wasn't right. As he emerged from the pool, he could feel his sister staring at him.

From the deck, he looked over the rest of the pool. Waves rolled in and lapped at the sides, but even from where he stood, Ben could see that the water was completely unoccupied. The only dark shapes were the five racing lanes that ran the length of the pool's bottom.

Ben picked up his towel, wiped his eyes, and dried his hair. He gave the water another quick scan.

Nothing.

"I think I'm done swimming for the night," Ben whispered to himself.

CHAPTER 3

NIGHTTIME VISITOR

Later that evening, Ben went into his room to start getting ready for bed. Between the long bus ride and their time in the pool, he was pretty exhausted. He decided to read his book for a while to relax. He wanted to get a good night's sleep before whatever adventures his grandparents had planned for them the next day.

He changed out of his swimsuit and spotted the pair of shorts he'd worn earlier in the day. After washing his hands, he found his toothbrush in his travel toiletry bag and a small tube of toothpaste. As he brushed his teeth, he looked in the mirror at his reflection. The Ben that stared back at him looked a little worn out and had foam coming out of his mouth like he had rabies or something.

Ben spit, rinsed a bit, and kept brushing. He'd heard singing the "Happy Birthday" song four times was about the amount of time a person should brush. It was something Ben tried doing out loud until Lola gave him a hard time for being a dork and getting toothpaste all over the mirror.

Instead, he just did it in his head. As he neared the end of his third run through the song, Ben tilted his head and spit again. When he looked up in the mirror, he could see a small boy standing near the bathtub, looking at him. Ben jumped back, dropping his toothbrush into the sink, splashing little spots of toothpaste everywhere.

Who is that? Ben's mind screamed as his heart ran a marathon inside his chest. He was almost afraid to move and held his breath, certain that if he did breathe, whatever it was he'd seen would get him.

He closed his eyes for a moment and listened, wondering if he'd hear his visitor's breathing or anything else. Other than the water running and the sound of the television in the living room, there was silence.

Ben opened his eyes and looked into the mirror again. There, standing silently in the shadow of the surrounding shower curtain of his grandparent's clawfoot tub, was a little boy. He was wearing a black coat, buttoned up the front over what looked like a plain white shirt. His hair looked messy, almost as though he

had just woken up from a night's sleep. From where he stood, it was difficult to see any details of his face. He looked almost fuzzy, like an out-of-focus photograph.

When it appeared that he could see Ben looking at him, he tilted his head down as if to hide his face.

There's someone in the bathroom, Ben thought. *Someone who doesn't belong in here. And worst of all? He sees me!*

Unsure what else to do, Ben turned his head to look at the boy directly. As soon as he did, the figure of the small boy was gone without a trace. Ben stood there staring at the spot next to the shower curtain for a full two minutes before he dared move another muscle. Whatever was there, if there was something there, was gone.

"Hello?" Ben whispered, almost afraid something might answer back. Other than the noise from the rest of the apartment, he couldn't hear anything.

Feeling a little more confident, he took a cautious step toward the bathtub, preparing himself for the little boy, or something else, to jump out at him from behind the shower curtain. Nothing did. He even reached out and brushed the curtain aside to make sure someone wasn't hiding there.

The tub was empty, and Ben was alone in the bathroom, just as he was supposed to be.

Am I seeing things? Ben wondered. When he blinked, he could see the faded image of the small boy for a split second. It was like it was almost burned into his memory.

He turned around to see if there was someone standing near the open door. Even though there was no room for anyone to hide behind it, he moved the door to check anyway. There was no one there, only a towel hanging from a hook.

Not wanting to be in the bathroom anymore, Ben rinsed his toothbrush quickly, turned off the faucet, and switched off the light. As he stepped into the hallway, he took another glance back into the bathroom.

Ben took a deep breath, prepared to see someone staring back at him.

The bathroom was empty.

————

Ben poked his head into Lola's room. His sister was lying on her side, facing away from the door. As usual she had her headphones in, watching a video on her phone. She never saw him come in, and when he tapped her on the shoulder, she jumped and nearly hit the ceiling.

"Hey!" Lola shouted. "What are you doing? You almost gave me a heart attack!"

Grandma shuffled into the bedroom.

"Are you two okay?" she asked. Her eyes glanced worriedly between the two of them.

"We're fine, Grandma," Lola insisted, swatting her brother on the shoulder. "Ben just startled me."

"Too much time with those headphones in," Grandma said with a sly wink. "You're going to miss out on real life."

Lola nodded, removed her headphones, and put them on the bedside table. Grandma seemed satisfied with this and left after delivering a quick kiss to each of their cheeks.

"I bet you have those back in your ears within ten minutes," Ben said. He was happy for the temporary distraction.

"Oh, be quiet," Lola groaned. "What do you want?"

Ben took a deep breath and glanced over his shoulder. Part of him didn't want his grandparents to hear, and the other part worried that something was watching him from the hallway.

"I saw something," Ben said carefully.

"Well, congratulations," Lola said. "I saw something too, Ben."

"Very funny," Ben said, shaking his head. He'd grown up with a smart aleck of a sister, and he'd walked right into that one. "No, I'm being serious. I saw something in the bathroom that shouldn't be there."

"Gross," Lola replied, but then her face changed as if she finally recognized that her brother wasn't messing around. "Okay, what's going on with you? Are you okay?"

Ben sat down on the end of the bed, and Lola sat up with her back against the headboard. She tossed her phone aside and stared at her older brother, waiting for him to spill what was happening.

"So," Ben began. "You're going to think I'm losing my mind or something, but I swear I saw someone in the bathroom with me."

"What do you mean?" Lola looked past him and into the hallway where the bathroom was, almost as if she expected to see someone and that would explain everything.

"There was a little boy in the bathroom," Ben whispered.

"Shut up," Lola said. "What? Why? How?"

"I'm serious," Ben said. "I was in there brushing my teeth, and when I looked in the mirror, I could see him behind me, standing by the tub."

"If you're messing with me . . . ," Lola began.

Ben felt her study his face for any signs that he was playing around.

"But you're not," she said quietly. "Is—is he still in there?"

"No," Ben said. "I turned around and he was gone, like he was never even there. I didn't hear footsteps, breathing, or anything. It's like he vanished."

Lola let that sink in for a moment. She crossed her arms as if refusing to believe anything Ben had told her. She even shook her head.

"Then you just saw something," Lola said. "Like a trick of the eye or whatever you want to call it. A figment."

"You think I just imagined it?" Ben asked.

"Well?" Lola said, throwing her hands up. "What else could it be? There's nothing there, and I can't imagine some little kid could just sneak into this apartment building, then take the elevator to the twenty-second floor, only to sit and watch you brush your choppers."

Ben snorted a bit. It did seem pretty ridiculous.

"Maybe I am seeing things," Ben said with a nervous laugh. "It doesn't make sense, does it?"

"Um, no," Lola said. "And between this and you seeing someone in the swimming pool earlier tonight, I'm beginning to think you're even weirder than I realized."

Ben felt his pulse quicken. He'd all but forgotten about the small figure he thought he'd seen at the bottom of the pool. It was hard to see through blurry, chlorinated eyes, but . . .

Had it been the same figure? Had it been the little boy too?

"I don't know what that was down there," Ben said. "But I swore I saw something."

Lola shrugged. "I don't know, man," she said. "None of us saw what you saw. And we definitely didn't see a little kid or anything."

Ben felt his arms prickle with goose bumps as if a wave of cold had washed past him. He rubbed his arms and smiled as best he could. There was no reason to think it was anything more than his imagination playing tricks on him. That was it.

"Okay," Ben said. "I'll leave you alone. Sorry to scare you before."

"Yeah, well?" Lola said. "You're a scary-looking guy, Ben."

"You're still not funny," Ben said. "Good night."

Ben stood up and went to his room and dug his book out from his bag. He turned on his bedside lamp and slipped under the covers, prepared to knock out a chapter or two before going to sleep. As he read and reread the first page over and over, he realized he was too distracted to focus on what he was reading.

I'm tired and worn out from the day, Ben assured himself. He remembered staying up all night at his friend Jonah's house last winter. By the time 4:00 a.m. rolled around, he could barely keep his eyes open, and when he did open them, he kept seeing things that weren't truly there.

He wasn't sure they were actual hallucinations but quickly learned that an exhausted mind couldn't be trusted.

So I'm tired, Ben thought. *That's what it is. Plain and simple.*

The only problem? Ben wasn't nearly as tired now as he had been that night. His body? Yes. His mind? Not so much.

With the plan to get as much sleep as possible, Ben turned out the light and closed his eyes.

CHAPTER 4

FIND ME

Ben wasn't sure how long he'd been asleep before he heard the voice. It was faint and hard to hear, almost like an ultra-whisper, but it was enough to make him open his eyes. He didn't dare do much more than that. He stayed completely still, trying to see as much as he could in the dark of his temporary bedroom.

There was a dim light coming from the main living area, likely from the kitchen. He waited a moment to listen, struggling to hear anything over the beating of his own heart and the light ringing in his ears. That happened anytime he was awoken from a nightmare. He wasn't sure *what* this was.

Ben couldn't hear whispering anymore, or anything else strange. His ears only caught the occasional ticking of appliances and the distant bubbling of his grandparents' fish tank in the living room.

He looked around the room to see if there was anything strange or out of place. Nothing seemed out of the ordinary. He could see his bag next to the dresser, a small bookshelf loaded with old photo albums, and a standing floor lamp.

"Hello?" Ben whispered so slightly he could barely hear himself. He didn't get any response.

Feeling a little less frightened, he turned from his side and onto his back and then froze, listening to see if there was another whisper.

Silence.

Oddly enough, there was a musty, almost fishy smell in the air. He'd almost assumed it was something his grandparents had been cooking, but remembered they'd had pizza for dinner.

Ben slowly sat up in his bed. As he did, he realized how chilly his room was. It was almost like sitting up in a cloud of cold. He was used to low temperatures during winters in Columbus, but not in an apartment during a Chicago summer.

Do Grandpa and Grandma really keep the air conditioning this low?

Come find me . . . A voice seemed to whisper directly into Ben's head. It was faint, but unmistakable. Someone was trying to talk to him, yet he didn't see anyone in the room.

"Lola?" Ben whimpered. "Knock it off! You're not funny!"

He was beginning to regret saying anything to his sister about the "visitor" he'd spotted in the bathroom and maybe at the bottom of the pool. Ben knew it would be just like her to pull a prank like this on him.

Ben waited for her eventual laugh, but when none came, he felt his heart beat a little faster.

"Lola? Seriously."

As soon as Ben said it, he could see someone peering at him from the doorway to his room. Ben backed up so that he was pressed against his headboard. It was too dark to make out any details, but he could see half of a figure. It was partially hidden by the doorframe and illuminated by the little light from the apartment's kitchen.

It seemed to peek at him from the hallway, watching him.

Who is that?! Ben's mind screamed. His beating heart felt like it might shatter his rib cage. He squinted, thinking it might help him see any details on the figure, but it didn't. When Ben flinched slightly, the figure moved left as if to slip back into the hallway.

Toward Lola's room.

It's definitely her, Ben thought, telling himself that was the only logical explanation.

With a newfound sense of bravery, he threw his blankets aside and hopped out of his bed. As soon as his feet hit the wood floor, a shiver ran up his spine. The floor was freezing, just like the air around him, making him wince a bit.

Ben walked out of his room and headed down the hall to Lola's room. He peered through her partially closed door to see her zonked out in her bed. Her mouth was partway open, and her arm was hanging over the side of her bed.

"Lola," he whispered.

She didn't stir. He opened the door slightly and could hear her heavy breathing that was just shy of a snore. He wouldn't put it past her to fake sleep, but something told him she was really down for the count. His sister, while kind of a pain at times, was no actor.

Just to be sure, he took one step into her room and realized that his bare foot went from cold to warm. It was strange. The hallway floor was as cold as it had been in his room, while Lola's floor . . . wasn't.

Before Ben could even consider how this was possible, he caught a movement to his right. He turned in time to see a figure disappear into the main living area. Ben froze for a second as if to process what he *thought* he'd seen.

Am I hallucinating? Or am I still dreaming?

He also noticed he could no longer smell the musty, fishy stink he'd picked up in his room. It was gone.

You're hearing and smelling things, he thought. *Just great.*

Ben moved away from his sister's door and took in his surroundings. It still felt cold, but he didn't see anything weird that would make him think he was stuck in a dream or even a nightmare. Everything looked like it did when the rest of his family was awake and the lights were on.

Knowing he couldn't spend his entire night in the hallway, he took three slow steps back toward his room, pausing at the doorway that led into the living room and kitchen.

"Hello?" Ben whispered. "Is there anybody out there?"

He would've been thrilled and relieved if his Grandpa answered back and said, "Just getting a late-night snack, Ben. Come join me."

That didn't happen.

Instead, he heard that unmistakable whisper that

didn't seem to come from any one direction, but from within himself.

Are you looking for me?

The voice, definitely childlike and definitely not Lola's, made Ben shudder. It sounded light and playful as if what it was doing wasn't even remotely creepy in the least. Ben wanted to jump back into bed and hide beneath the covers. Instead, he found himself walking into the living room as if he could face whoever was whispering to him head-on.

"Where are you?" Ben asked, bracing himself for the bone-chilling whisper he was sure would follow. Instead, he felt cold again like he had in his room. The air smelled fishy out here too.

You have to find me, came the faint, breathy whisper. It sounded farther away, as if the voice itself was trying to hide from him too.

Ben stood in the living room and paused for a moment. He blinked a few times in an attempt to somehow reset his brain. He was having a conversation with a strange voice in the middle of the night, and he felt like he was one second away from screaming and waking up the rest of the apartment building.

I have to be dreaming, Ben thought, unable to come up with any other valid explanation.

He looked across the open area, scanning the large island in the kitchen with stools positioned around it. He glanced across the dining room table, slowing to see if he could see anyone or anything beneath the chairs.

Nothing seemed out of order.

Ben turned to his right to look over the living room with the sectional couch, ottoman, and end tables. He spotted his grandpa's Cubs hat on the seat of the recliner he seemed to like best. The large shelving unit with countless old books and trinkets from Japan adorning the shelves appeared undisturbed. He glanced over to the large fish tank.

That fishy smell, Ben thought. *Was it from there?*

As he watched the three koi fish his grandparents had in the tank, he saw a face looking back at him through the dark glass. It was the face of the boy he'd seen in the bathroom. He had messy brown hair, and his eyes, though shadowed, looked right into Ben's.

"What is that?" Ben whispered.

At the sound of his voice, the boy seemed to lower his head as if trying to keep his face hidden from Ben. He almost disappeared, keeping his eyes above the layer of small rocks at the bottom of the aquarium.

"Who are you?" Ben asked, struggling to keep his voice from shaking in fear. He knew he was probably too young to have a heart attack, but he felt close to one.

Instead of an answer, he could hear laughing. It was the sound of a young boy giggling at something. To Ben, standing in his grandparents' cold apartment at who-knows-when in the morning, it was the most unsettling sound he'd heard in a long time.

Even so, he found himself walking toward the fish tank. His mind was screaming for him to stop, but his body was pressing on anyway. Ben found himself helpless to do anything but move closer and closer. As he did, the young boy's face slid farther behind the tank as if wanting to hide himself.

After a few more steps, Ben was able to glance behind the tank. The lights from the city outside made it just bright enough to see that there was no one there.

His breath came out in a relieved rush, but he was left wondering who the boy was and where he'd gone.

"Hello?" Ben called, a little louder than he should have.

As he stood there, scanning the room to find the strange boy, he felt the room warm and the fishy smell disappear. He didn't see the little boy anymore and was both relieved and confounded. He had no idea where the kid could have gone, where he'd come from, or if he was going to show up again.

I have to get back to bed or wake up, Ben thought. *Did any of this actually happen? Am I just seeing things?*

He carefully made his way back to his room, checking and rechecking any possible place where the boy might be hiding. When he stepped into the hallway, a hand touched his shoulder.

Ben cried out and jerked away. A moment later the hallway light was switched on.

"Benji?"

"Grandpa." Ben let out a shuddering gasp. "You scared me."

"Scared me too," he said. "I heard you calling for someone. Were you sleepwalking?"

Ben thought about telling him about the boy but couldn't find words that didn't sound absolutely ridiculous. Instead, he shrugged and scratched his head.

"I don't know what I was doing," he admitted, which wasn't too far from the truth.

"It's very late," Grandpa said, patting him on the shoulder. "You need to get plenty of rest. We have a big day tomorrow."

Ben let his grandpa guide him into his bedroom and lay there while his grandpa got him tucked in like he had when Ben was much younger. It made him feel safe, at least for the moment.

Feeling calm, Ben said good night to his grandpa and told him he'd see him in the morning. When his grandpa left the room, he turned to his side. As his eyes started to close, he noticed something shiny on his nightstand.

It was the little metal boat. The one he'd left in the bathroom earlier in the evening.

His heart thumped in growing terror until he told himself something to calm his mind.

Someone else probably found it and brought it into my room. I'm not the only one to use the bathroom, and everyone knows I was the one who found it.

As he closed his eyes, the same voice he'd heard earlier faintly whispered, *Why haven't they found me?*

CHAPTER 5

BOAT TRIP

The next morning at breakfast, Ben was the last one to sit down at the kitchen island. When he did, the others stared at him as if he had grown another head overnight. Too tired to question it, Ben just took a bite of his breakfast burrito. But it was only a matter of time before his sister piped up.

"Okay," Lola said. "I'm going to say it. You look terrible, Ben."

"Thanks," Ben replied, before taking a sip of his orange juice.

"Those movies where zombies come out of graves to eat the faces of the living?" Lola said. "That's what you look like."

"I look like the zombies or the people without a face?" Ben asked.

"Yes," Lola replied.

"Great," Ben replied.

He'd found in the past the best thing to do when Lola was on a roll was to just ignore her and not respond.

He knew saying anything would just encourage her to keep being snarky.

"Are you okay?" Grandpa asked. He held his mug of tea close to his lips to blow the steam away.

"Yeah, I just didn't sleep well," Ben said. Grandpa winked at him as though they shared a secret. He had found him wandering around in the dark last night, after all.

"Oh no. Was the bed uncomfortable, Ben?" Grandma asked.

Ben looked up at his grandma and saw her face was drawn in worry.

"No," Ben replied. "It was super comfortable. I just—"

He looked over at Lola who had her eyebrows raised in anticipation.

"—I just have a hard time getting used to a different bed, that's all," Ben said.

"I'm so sorry," Grandma said. "Maybe you can take a nap later?"

He wasn't sure how much sleep he'd gotten the night before, but it wasn't much. He didn't have the heart to tell them that something strange was going on in their new home. Maybe he was overthinking things, but he didn't want to be disrespectful.

Even so, he couldn't help but hear the last thing the voice had said to him.

Why haven't they found me?

If the little kid—whatever he was—was playing hide-and-seek, Ben had sort of played it with him, having found him behind the fish aquarium. So who was this "they" he was talking about?

As he bit off another bite of his burrito, he looked over at the fish tank, where his grandparents' fish were slowly gliding back and forth through the water. He half expected to see the boy's face staring back at him through the glass.

Ben shuddered.

"You don't have to take a nap," Grandma said, making him realize she must've been waiting for a response from him.

"Sorry," Ben said "Just kind of zoning out. I'll be fine, Grandma, really."

Really? he asked himself. *Will I really?*

"Well, we've got a reservation with the tour boat in about an hour," Grandpa said, looking at his watch.

Ben nodded. He thought the best thing for him would be to get out of the apartment for a while. Maybe he just needed some fresh air and a river cruise to occupy his brain. At least, he hoped so.

———————

A little later that morning, they were boarding the *Chicago Princess*, a large boat with two levels, the upper level for those wanting an open-air experience. Ben's family agreed that sitting up top and in the sun was the way to go.

He followed his grandparents upstairs and saw there were plenty of places for them to sit. They sat behind a family with German accents who had two young twin girls. They turned and looked at Ben and his grandparents. His grandma smiled and waved at them until the girls became too embarrassed and turned around in their seats.

In a matter of minutes, more than half of the seats were filled, and the tour was ready to begin. Grandpa leaned close to Ben and whispered, "You doing okay, Ben?"

Ben nodded. Being out in the sun and the fresh air did make him feel a little better, even if the air did have a funky river smell to it. It was strange to be in a boat in the middle of the city and see skyscrapers and cars driving back and forth.

As the boat's engines fired up, a woman in a bright-red vest stood up at the front of the boat. She held a microphone and studied it. A moment later there was a loud screech of audio feedback.

"Sorry about that," the woman said with a big bright smile. There was a large space between her teeth. "Sometimes this thing likes to yell at me."

The crowd seemed to think that was funny, and she continued on, introducing herself as Karen and letting everyone know she would be their guide for the Chicago River architecture tour. She pointed out that everyone needed to silence their phones but said they were welcome to take photos and video of the tour.

"Let's get this party started, shall we?" Karen said, and most of the crowd clapped their hands. Some guy in the back whistled.

Ben listened as Karen started off the tour with details about the river itself. He learned it wasn't a completely naturally made river, but a series of canals and rivers and swamps that fed into Lake Michigan. Through a lot of hard work, engineers had been able to reverse the direction the river flowed so that water from the Great Lake fed the Chicago River and its tributaries.

"Here's a fun fact," Karen said. "The city's namesake, 'Chicago' comes from an Algonquin word for wild onion."

An older lady with white curly hair raised her hand.

"Yes!" Karen cried, seemingly excited to call on the woman. "You have a question?"

"Why onions?" the woman asked, lifting her head up to receive the answer.

"So glad you asked, ma'am," Karen replied. "Wild onions used to grow in abundance in the smelly swamps and bogs that were here before the Windy City was built up to what it's become today."

Ben watched as they passed numerous old buildings and listened to the dates they were built and how long they'd taken to be completed. He watched as his sister took pictures of the city and turned to take a selfie with Ben and the grandparents.

"Squish in, guys," Lola said, making sure she fit all of them into the frame.

Ben was sure he looked really great, running on only a couple hours of sleep. He knew he'd hear about it later when Lola looked through her camera roll.

As they continued down the river, he noticed that the buildings and architecture looked somewhat familiar. When they passed underneath the bridge for LaSalle Boulevard, Ben realized where they were.

"Isn't that your apartment building, Grandpa?"

"It sure is," he replied. "But I doubt they'll talk about it since it's so new. Only old stuff is interesting on these tours."

As the boat ventured beneath the bridge, the boat slowed and Karen took a somber tone.

"It's here we're going to talk about one of the great tragedies that happened in this very section of the river," Karen said. "On July 24, 1915, there was a boat accident that claimed the lives of more passengers than the sinking of the *Titanic*."

There were murmurs in the crowd. Ben even heard one man say, "I didn't know that."

As if she could hear him, Karen continued on. "If you hadn't heard about the SS *Eastland* before, you're not alone. There were two thousand five hundred people onboard, which included both passengers and the crew. The boat was a passenger ship that was bound for Michigan City, Indiana, for the Western Electric Company's annual picnic."

"What happened?" Ben whispered to his grandfather, who shook his head slightly to show that he didn't even know himself.

The entire boat listened in silence as Karen explained that the ship had capsized, tipping over right into the river. Since there were many people already inside and below decks, they were trapped as the water rushed in.

"They never even left the dock," Karen said. "People who were there to watch from the shore did what they could to save as many of the passengers as possible, but eight hundred forty-four people died during what is now known as the *Eastland* disaster."

Ben looked around. It was hard to imagine a boat sinking so close to shore and losing that many people to such a strange accident. People were asking questions, but he found it hard to concentrate. He wondered why pretty much everyone knew about the *Titanic*, but he'd never heard of the SS *Eastland*. It was like the people who died in the tragedy had been forgotten.

"People worked as quickly as they could," Karen said. "But time ran short, and some couldn't be reached in time. Twenty-two entire families were gone in a matter of moments. Because there were so many, they brought the recovered bodies to the Second Regiment Armory nearby."

Their guide explained how they had laid all of the bodies on the floor inside the armory to try and identify the deceased, using it as a makeshift morgue.

Ben felt himself not wanting to hear any more and glanced over at his sister. She listened in horror, covering her mouth with her hand. Though she could be a little sassy at times, Lola took sad stories to heart and looked upset by what she was hearing.

He watched her turn to their grandma and mouth the words, *It's just so sad.*

As Karen apologized for bringing the mood on the boat down, she told them that she felt it important for everyone onboard to know the river's history, good and bad. As the boat picked up speed again to continue on the last leg of the tour, something caught Ben's eye.

In a row of empty seats, a small boy stood, looking over the railing and down into the river.

Ben felt his breath hide in his throat as he immediately recognized the kid.

He leaned back and reached behind his grandparents to tap his sister on the shoulder. Lola leaned her head back and looked at Ben with a puzzled expression.

What? she mouthed.

"He's here," Ben whispered, and nodded toward the front of the boat.

His sister turned her head and gazed forward, and he did too. He pointed in the direction where he'd seen the boy, only to discover he'd disappeared.

Of course he did, Ben thought.

He rubbed his tired eyes and watched his sister scan the boat, as if still trying to find the mysterious boy her older brother kept talking about. Ben exhaled in frustration. He didn't know how he could expect anyone to believe him when the strange kid kept disappearing on him.

It was almost as if . . .

"Ben? You feeling all right?" Grandpa said. "You look like you've just seen a ghost."

He stood up quickly and whispered that he needed

to use the bathroom. As if seeing that he wasn't doing well, Grandpa got up too.

"I'll go with you," he said.

"I'm okay," Ben said, his head swirling a bit, making him feel dizzy. "I just need to get up for a second."

His grandfather insisted on following him, walking with him downstairs to help him find the restroom. He could hear Karen talking about the architecture of the Clark Street Bridge through the boat's speakers as he opened the men's room door.

"I'll wait out here, Benji," Grandpa said.

Ben could barely hear him. All he could do was close the door behind him, lock it, and look at himself in the mirror. He stared at his reflection for a moment and saw his grandpa was right.

I look like I've seen a ghost.

CHAPTER 6

THROW BACK

The bus ride back to his grandparents' apartment was a blur to Ben. He kept seeing flashes of the boy on the boat, staring into the river. No one else had seemed to notice him, and just like before, he had disappeared before Ben could point him out.

Is the kid really a ghost? Ben wondered. *And is he following me?*

"Can you hear me, Ben?" Grandma asked, sort of jolting him back to reality.

"What?" Ben said. "I'm sorry. Yes."

"Are you okay?" Grandma asked. Her voice was still kind and patient, but there was concern written all over her face.

"I don't know," Ben admitted.

"Do you feel sick?" Grandpa asked. "Like you might throw up?"

Ben shook his head. He wasn't sure if he was sick, but he didn't feel like he was going to barf all over the place. Sure, he looked pale and messed up, but it was more his head that felt wrong, not his stomach.

"I'm sorry," Ben said. "I just thought I saw something, and I don't know if it was real or not."

Grandma and Grandpa looked at each other. Lola even looked a little worried, which was rare for her.

"What did you see?" Grandma asked.

"It was a little boy," Ben admitted. "Maybe five years old or something. But when I looked again, he wasn't there."

"On the boat?"

Ben nodded. He almost mentioned that he'd seen him at their apartment too but then didn't.

"There were a few kids on the boat," Grandma said. "Maybe he was one of them?"

"I don't know," Ben said. "Maybe? Or maybe I'm just tired."

The group was quiet for a moment as the bus continued down the city streets, toward his grandparents' apartment building.

"We'll have a quiet night tonight," Grandma said, putting her arm around Ben. "Let you relax and catch up on your sleep."

"That sounds great," Ben said, but deep down the

thought of going to sleep was actually a little scary to him.

As they reached their bus stop, Ben glanced at the new apartment building on West Wacker Drive.

There's no way a new building like that could be haunted, could it? he wondered. Weren't haunted places old and falling apart?

————————

That night his grandparents made miso soup, reminding both Lola and Ben that no one made a better dinner than their grandparents. After they were finished and cleared the dishes, they settled down to watch a movie, keeping their promise of a nice quiet evening inside.

Ben grabbed the "comfy spot" on the large sectional couch, wedged into the corner so he could put his legs up and nestle in. Lola sat on the end, demanding that she get to pick the movie since she didn't get to sit where she wanted.

"Knock yourself out," Ben said. "If you pick something boring enough, I'll go right to sleep."

Lola didn't disappoint. She chose a movie about a girl who finds a magical horse that can both fly and talk. No one looked excited to watch it, but they rented it, and in moments, the movie began.

Sometime between the opening credits and the third or fourth scene, Ben felt his eyes get heavy. He only thought about the boy on the boat once and wondered if seeing the ghost on the boat meant the kid had moved on.

Maybe he wasn't haunting the apartment anymore, Ben thought. *Maybe he'll leave me alone.*

Feeling hopeful, Ben let the movie he had zero interest in lull him to sleep.

———————

The sound of something like a metallic tap on the glass made Ben wake up. When he did, he had no idea how long he'd been asleep. He sat up, confused by his surroundings, and looked around. He wasn't in his bedroom back in Ohio or his bedroom for the weekend in Chicago.

He was in his grandparents' living room, and from the looks of it, he'd successfully slept through the entire movie, *Magic Mare*. The rest of the apartment was dark, save for the lights under the cabinets and the lights of the buildings outside the windows. Someone had put a thin blanket over him.

They let me sleep out here, Ben thought, looking around. *Probably afraid to wake me up.*

He squinted at the microwave and saw the blue digital numbers on the front read 11:42. It was hard to believe he'd pretty much slept for at least five hours.

Ben rubbed his eyes and spotted something on the glass coffee table positioned in front of the sectional. There, sitting upright and next to a collection of coasters, was the small metal boat. He didn't know how it had gotten there, but he wasn't happy to see it.

Did Lola put it there? Grandma or Grandpa? Ben wondered. Did they think he needed it to go to sleep or something?

Seeing it sitting on the table made him feel uneasy.

Ben sat forward and picked it up. It felt, like it always had, cold to the touch. He wasn't sure if it was because of the metal or what. Regardless, he felt the sudden urge to get rid of the thing. Without stopping to question why, Ben stood up and walked to the kitchen. He made his way to the stainless steel garbage can and set his bare foot on the bar at the base. The lid popped up, and he dropped the little boat on top of the trash inside. It fell to the bottom with a satisfying *clunk*.

Almost instantly, he felt better, as if a weight had been lifted.

Ben lifted his foot and the garbage can lid closed.

Feeling good, he went into the bathroom and brushed his teeth. He glanced into the mirror to see if the boy was watching him from the shower curtain again and saw no one. He spit, rinsed, and checked the mirror again.

No one.

After finishing up in the bathroom, he went into

his bedroom to finish the night sleeping in a bed. He clicked on the light so that he could change into his pajamas and froze in place.

There, sitting below his lamp, was the small metal boat.

You have got to be kidding me, Ben thought, his mind and heart racing. *How is this possible?*

He knew it couldn't have been Lola or his grandparents who had moved it. The house had been silent. Plus he'd had the door to the bathroom open. The boy did it. There was no other explanation.

Now, more than ever, he wanted to get rid of the boat. For good.

Ben grabbed the little boat and walked out into the living room. He didn't stop to look to see if the boy was trying to play hide-and-seek with him again. Even if he was, Ben wasn't playing. He unlocked the apartment unit's front door, opened it, and flipped the dead bolt. Very carefully, he let it come to rest on the doorframe, a precaution to keep him from being locked out.

Moving quickly, he took the elevator down to the main floor and entered the lobby. The large area was dim and quiet. Ben headed for the front door. The automatic doors slid open, and he was out onto the sidewalk in his bare feet. Looking both ways, he crossed West Wacker Drive and made his way to the sidewalk that ran parallel to the Chicago River.

He looked at the little boat one last time. Ben didn't care if it was an antique or worth a ton of money. He didn't want anything to do with the boat or the boy that seemed somehow attached to it.

"Bon voyage," Ben said, and threw the little boat as far as he could into the water. The sounds of the city drowned out the tiny splash it made, but he instantly felt better.

Realizing it was dangerous to be out in the city on his own and at a ridiculous hour, he made his way back across the street, up to the twenty-second floor, and back into his grandparents' apartment. He locked the door behind him, went to his room, and got dressed for bed.

Feeling free of the cursed little boat, Ben quickly fell asleep.

Sometime after closing his eyes that night, Ben dreamed.

In his dream, he was walking through a dimly lit hallway. His footsteps echoed through the space, but there wasn't anyone else around. Old doors with metal knobs were closed on either side of him. Up ahead was a set of large double doors.

Ben walked up to the doors and turned the knobs on both, pushing them forward and open into a much larger room.

The room he stepped into was considerably brighter and more open. The ceilings were far above his head, with sunlight seeming to pour in from large openings somewhere high above. He stopped and looked around the room, certain he'd never seen a place like it before.

There were men in dark-blue uniforms standing around items lined up on the ground. They wore dark hats and shiny badges on the fronts of their coats. It didn't take Ben long to realize the men were police officers, but they looked different from the ones he was used to. They were from another time.

An older time.

Ben walked forward and saw that there were hundreds of things laid out on the ground, but almost all were completely covered up. Some were short. Some were longer. Others seemed larger than the others.

One of the police officers crouched and pulled the sheet back a bit. Beneath it Ben could see the pale face of a woman with her eyes closed.

Bodies, Ben thought. *All of these "things" lying on the ground are bodies.*

He looked around and realized that there were hundreds and hundreds of them. Though he didn't want to get closer, Ben found himself walking toward them, watching the police study the collection of bodies laid out on the floor of the massive room.

I don't want to be here, Ben thought, but his body didn't listen. It kept walking forward. Soon it was walking between the rows of them, inches away from the covered corpses. The police didn't seem to notice or mind that he was there, instead continuing their investigation. Another man stood by with a clipboard, writing something down.

As Ben continued down, he noticed movement to his right. One of the bodies was sitting up. The higher it rose, the more the sheet that covered it slipped. In a matter of seconds, the covering revealed the face of a young boy that was all too familiar to Ben.

Ready or not, the boy seemed to say without moving his mouth, *here I come.*

———

Ben bolted straight up in his bed, panting as if he'd just completed a race. He gripped his blankets tight and looked around, certain he'd see a figure watching him from the shadows. His eyes darted around the room looking for any sign.

There wasn't one.

I know that place, Ben thought. His mind gave him quick flashes of the room and the rows and rows of bodies. *It was the armory. The place where they put all of the bodies they pulled out of the Chicago River. Somehow I was able to see it.*

"It doesn't mean anything," Ben whispered to himself, struggling to get his pounding heart and breathing under control. "It was just a dream. Just a dream."

He leaned over and turned on his bedside lamp.

There, sitting on the end table, next to his book, was the tiny metal boat.

CHAPTER 7

NIGHT TALKERS

Ben didn't remember shouting out loud, but he must have, because a moment later his bedroom door creaked slightly.

"Whoa!" Lola said. "Take it easy. You're going to wake up everyone else too."

She stepped into his room in her pajamas. Her eyes looked sleepy, and there was a large line across her cheek. She looked like she'd maybe slept on the fold on a pillowcase or something. Her hair was messy too, sticking up and tangled in places.

Ben pressed his palms into his eyes for a moment. He hoped it would reset his brain somehow. When he moved them away, it truly was his sister standing at the end of his bed, looking at him like he'd just dropped out of a spacecraft.

"What is going on with you?" she asked, her face slowly coming back from a deep sleep. "I heard you cry out and . . ."

Ben turned and pointed at the little boat on the bedside table, silvery and motionless.

Lola walked over and looked down at the boat.

"So," she said slowly. "You're terrified of a toy boat."

"No," Ben whispered.

"I swear you're getting stranger by the day, Ben," Lola said. "What's going on with you?"

Ben took a deep breath and glanced at the floor. It was hard not to get frustrated with his little sister, especially when she was trying to be funny, usually at his expense. When he could see she was done with her comedy routine, he looked up at her.

"I think this little toy boat is cursed or something," Ben said quietly.

"Cursed?"

"Just listen for a second and let me try to explain," Ben said, trying his best to be patient with her.

"Fine." Lola sat at the end of the bed.

"Ever since I found this thing on the ground, weird things have been happening," Ben explained. "First I thought I saw someone or something in the pool with us on Thursday night."

Lola yawned. Ben gave her a dirty look.

"What? I'm tired," she said with a shrug. "It's not because your story is boring."

"You think this is boring?" Ben asked, shaking his head in disbelief. "Really?"

"No, no," Lola said. "That's not what I meant. Listen, I know something is bothering you, and I'm listening. It's not boring at all, okay? Just weird."

Ben continued.

"That night I saw that boy in the bathroom," he said. "Remember how I told you about him?" He didn't wait for her to answer. "Even later, in the middle of the night, I heard a voice and saw him behind the aquarium, like he was trying to hide from me or something."

Lola seemed to take this all in.

"You were up in the middle of the night? Chasing him around?"

Ben nodded.

"So, where is this kid? I mean, how is he getting into the apartment?" Lola asked.

"That's just it," Ben said. "I don't think he's real."

Her eyebrows were mashed together above her nose in confusion. "What?"

Ben took a deep breath and let it out as if preparing himself for a tough talk.

"I think this kid I'm seeing is a ghost," he said. "He's shown up a couple of times here, and I've heard his voice."

Lola stared at her brother.

"What did he say?" Lola asked. Ben could feel her eyes burn into him, as if waiting for him to say he was just messing with her or for the inevitable joke that was only seconds away.

"He said things like *Come find me* and—"

"'Come find me'?" Lola repeated.

"Yeah," Ben said. It's almost like he was trying to play hide-and-seek with me or something. It's—"

"Super creepy," Lola finished. "But doesn't that seem kind of impossible? I mean, do you think this apartment building is haunted or something?"

Ben shrugged.

"I don't know," he admitted. "This place seems too new to have ghosts running around, but I don't know how all of that works. I'm not even sure I believe ghosts are real. At least I didn't before yesterday."

Lola looked around the room as if she might be able to spot the ghost for herself.

"Is he in here right now?" Lola asked quietly. "Do you see him?"

"No," Ben said, his eyes darting around the room. "But I don't think he's too far away."

Ben leaned to the left to look past his sister and out into the hallway. There was a creak in the floor.

"Is that him?" Lola whispered. "He knows we're talking about him."

Her eyes were wide with fear.

At that moment, a figure appeared in the doorway.

Lola turned and gasped, making Ben jump too.

"Grandma!" Ben whisper-shouted. "You startled us."

"Funny," Grandma replied, clutching the front of her robe. "You startled me. What are you two doing awake?"

Ben looked at Lola, and she shook her head at him slightly.

"I made some noise and startled Lola," Ben said, keeping his answer truthful. "So we're just talking until we get tired again."

"Yeah," Lola said. "Sorry if we woke you up."

Grandma gave them both a tired smile. "I'm just glad to see you getting along," she said. "Don't stay up too much longer."

"We won't," Lola said. "Good night."

Grandma gave both of them a hug and headed back to bed.

"I'm glad I haven't said anything," Ben said. "They'd feel really bad if we told them I think this place is haunted."

"No kidding," Lola said. She glanced toward the lamp and down at the boat. "So what's the deal with this boat? You said you think it's cursed?"

Ben looked at the small antique toy and exhaled. He kind of wanted to forget about it.

"Okay," he said. "Here's where you're going to think I'm crazy."

"Crazier?" Lola said. "Maybe."

"I'm serious," Ben said. "This might be the freakiest thing I've ever had happen in my life."

Lola looked at the boat, at her brother, and then back again. She gave herself a hug as if she was suddenly cold.

"Would you just tell me already?"

Ben swallowed and tried to think of the best way to explain. "Tonight when we were watching your ridiculous movie—"

"Hey," Lola interrupted.

"When I fell asleep, you guys left me in there, right?"

"Yeah," Lola said. "You were completely zonked out. Even the sounds of *Magic Mare* on the TV weren't waking you up. Grandpa thought it was best to just let you sleep through the night."

Ben recalled what it was that had stirred him from sleep.

"A noise actually woke me up," Ben said slowly, reliving the moment in his head. "It sounded like something hard hitting the glass table in the living room. I woke up and saw that toy boat on the coffee table."

"Shut up," Lola said. "Maybe you put it there."

"What?"

"I don't know," Lola said, rubbing her arms even

more vigorously. "You could've woken and picked it up and brought it back and . . ."

Ben stared at his sister with his eyebrows raised.

"Okay," she said. "Probably far-fetched. So what, then? You think—"

"I think the little boy brought it from my room out into the living room," Ben said. "I think it belongs to him."

Lola nodded and squinted at the little boat like she was studying it from afar.

"So get this," Ben said. "I was so freaked out by the thing that I picked it up and tossed it in the garbage. The one in the kitchen."

"Oh boy," Lola said.

"I went to the bathroom, brushed my teeth, and when I came into the bedroom . . ." Ben trailed off.

"There it was," Lola whispered. "Freaky."

Ben took a really deep breath. "It gets better," he said.

"I'm never going to sleep again, am I?" Lola asked.

"You don't want me to tell you?"

"Yes," Lola said. "No. Yes, yes. Just tell me."

Ben explained how he had grabbed the boat, gone downstairs, run across the street, and hurled it into the river. He'd come back upstairs, feeling better, and gone right to sleep. He told her about the dream and seeing the bodies laid out in the makeshift morgue.

"Never mind all that," Lola said. "You just told me you threw this little boat into the river. How did it get back here?"

"I woke up from the nightmare, and there it was, sitting right where you see it," Ben said. "As if I'd never thrown it as far away from here as I could. It was just sitting here, waiting for me."

Lola covered her mouth and shook her head.

"If you're making all of this up, I swear I'll never speak to you again."

"I'm not," Ben said. "No lie. When I saw it, I must've cried out or something. I don't know. I can't believe it's back here. I'm not even sure how it's possible."

Ben thought about it as his sister seemed to process what he'd told her.

Did the ghost boy follow me outside and find the boat down in the depths of the Chicago River? Can ghosts even carry stuff?

Lola leaned forward and reached for the boat. Ben watched as she hesitated a moment, as if unsure she should touch it. After a second or two, she picked it up, holding it in her hand. He could see her shiver once, as if a cold jolt went through her.

"Maybe it's not the apartment that's haunted," Lola said. "Maybe this thing is haunting you."

Ben hadn't thought of that, but he did think of something else just then. "Yeah? Well now that you touched it, maybe it's going to haunt you too."

"Oh," Lola said. "Great." She pretended she was going to throw it across the room, but didn't.

"That won't do any good," Ben said. "It'll just end up back here."

Lola laughed a little, and so did Ben.

"Whoa," she said. "We must be tired. We're holding a haunted boat and making dumb jokes. We should be screaming and scared of our own shadows."

"That's tomorrow," Ben said. "After the Cubs game."

"Well, that's good news," Lola said. "I can't imagine that little boy is going to follow you to Wrigley Field, right?"

"I don't know," Ben said. "I saw him on the boat earlier today."

"What?" Lola said. "You didn't tell me that."

"I tried to on the boat," Ben said. "Remember?"

Lola shook her head. "I thought you were pointing

at the lady with the weird hat sitting in front of us," she said. "How was I supposed to know you saw a ghost?"

Ben stared at Lola's hands. She was turning the toy boat in her hands. As she did, Ben thought about what the boy was doing on the riverboat.

"It's weird," he said. "When I saw him, he was just staring down into the water, as if he'd lost something. He didn't seem to care that I was there or even want to play hide-and-seek."

"He lost something, maybe," Lola said. "It can't be this boat, though. You found it, and he seems to want you to have it."

As Ben sat there, he felt his heartbeat quicken and his mind start to put the pieces together. He remembered where along the tour they had been when he spotted the kid, and a shiver raced down the back of his neck.

"Maybe he was one of the victims of the SS *Eastland* tragedy," Ben whispered, mostly to himself. "What if that's what this is all about? The river, the dream I had about the morgue. Maybe this kid is trying to tell me something."

Lola looked down at the boat in her hands, nodding slightly.

"I just wish I knew who this kid was and what he wanted from me," Ben said. "Besides playing the creepiest game of hide-and-seek ever."

"Well," Lola said, holding the boat close to her face. "If this boat truly belonged to him, I think we know his initials."

Before Ben could say anything, she held the bottom of the boat out to his face. There, scratched in the bottom, were two letters:

R. S.

CHAPTER 8

PREGAME

Both Lola and Ben ended up sleeping in his room that night. His sister snuck into her own room and snatched her pillows. Then she set herself up at the opposite end of his bed. Besides having her feet near his face and vice versa, it was a good setup.

Neither of them wanted to be alone in case the boy showed up again.

They slept through the night without incident, and Ben wondered if it was because Lola was in the same room with him.

Was the little boy afraid of her? Ben thought. Whatever it was, he left them alone, allowing Ben to get a good chunk of restful sleep for a change.

After breakfast the four of them spent the morning exploring the east end of the city, walking around Navy Pier and riding on the giant Ferris wheel there.

As they rose up into the sky in the ride's enclosed cabin, both Ben and Lola were wowed by the view of Lake Michigan.

"It's like an ocean," Lola said, getting as close to the glass as she could.

Ben sat still in his seat, enjoying the view from where he was. He didn't love heights and kept reminding himself that there was little chance any of them would fall out.

After a while they meandered back into the city. They needed to catch a ride north to Wrigley Field. When they reached the corner of State and Grand, Grandpa led them to a set of stairs.

"Hey, don't we need to catch a bus?" Lola asked.

"You actually want to take another bus ride?" Ben asked.

"We're going to take the L," Grandma said, pointing to where their grandfather was standing.

"The L?" Lola asked. "What does that even mean? It looks like he's going to go into the basement of the city."

Ben remembered seeing the trains and tracks above them in different parts of the city. He realized that they weren't going to bus their way to the stadium at all.

"Oh, so it's like a subway," Ben said. "Does the train take us right there?"

"It does," Grandma said with a smile. "Nice and quick."

The rest of the group followed Grandpa and descended the stairs into the underground station. It was brighter and busier than Ben expected—but a little confusing with staircases, turnstiles, and machines to buy passes.

Already prepared, Grandpa scanned his transit card four times, and they were on the platform within a matter of minutes. He glanced at his watch, just as the northbound train made its way out of the tunnel.

"Is that our ride?" Lola asked. "Is that the L?"

Grandpa nodded and adjusted his Cubs cap as the train came to a stop in front of them. The string of train cars was a lot longer than Ben would have guessed—he counted eight.

The four of them let the people get out of the train first and then headed in and found a group of seats together. There was a voice coming through the speakers that Ben could barely understand. He guessed it was announcing the next stop or that the train was going to be leaving soon, he wasn't sure.

As people scrambled to make the train, the doors along the side slid closed.

After another blurb on the loudspeaker, the train

started to move, heading away from the brightly lit station and into the dark tunnel ahead.

"Do you two know why the train is called the L?" Grandma asked looking across Grandpa at the two of them.

"No idea," Lola said. "Because the rest of the alphabet was taken?"

Grandma shook her head. "Good guess, but no. It's a nickname for the train system, short for 'elevated railroad.'"

"L, as in elevated," Ben said, nodding. "Makes sense."

"Not really," Lola said, looking around as the dark walls of the tunnel whipped past the windows. "We're not exactly elevated right now."

"We will be," Grandma said with a smile and a wink.

———

After a few more stops, the train emerged from the tunnel and the tracks rose up to truly elevate the L. Ben and Lola looked around as traffic from the streets moved beneath them and city neighborhoods whizzed by.

As they continued north along the tracks, Ben looked away from the window and toward the front of the train. He could see the back of a man wearing a hooded sweatshirt and big headphones. Sitting next to him was a young girl with colorful beads strung through her hair. Across the aisle Ben saw something that made his heart feel like it might stop.

There, peering at him from behind the white-and-blue seat, was a boy. His small hands were holding the top of the seat, but his head and face were lowered so that only his eyes were showing. Though it was perfectly bright outside, the boy looked faded, almost out of focus.

Though it was difficult to see his eyes, what Ben could see as the light and shadows flickered past his face was that his eyes looked empty.

And dead.

"Lola," Ben whispered.

He gently elbowed her in the side to draw her attention away from the window. When she turned, he held a finger over his mouth to keep her from saying anything too loudly.

"What's going on?" she asked quietly.

"He's here," Ben said under his breath. "Up ahead, at the front of the car."

He watched his sister, keeping his eyes on the side of her face. Something told him that she'd wear a confused look and tell him that she couldn't see the ghost boy. He was pretty certain that he would be the only one to ever see the apparition.

Her eyes narrowed.

"I see him," Lola whispered. "At least I think I do."

Ben looked back toward the boy. As he did, the boy slunk down behind his seat again, keeping all but his messy hair and clutching fingers from showing.

"That's him," Ben said.

He glanced at his grandparents. They were both looking at Grandpa's phone, trying to figure out where their game seats were on an online stadium map.

"You're sure?" Lola asked. "It's not just some little kid playing peek-a-boo with you or something?"

Ben looked at the kid again. As scared as he'd been over the last few days, he didn't feel frightened anymore. It was still really unsettling, but he didn't feel like the ghost, or whatever the kid truly was, meant to hurt him.

A hand clapped down on Ben's shoulder, making him jump slightly. He turned to see Grandpa smiling next to him.

"You're still a little jumpy," his grandfather said.

"Yeah," Ben laughed. "I guess I am."

"We're just about here," Grandpa said, and pointed out the window.

Coming up on the left, he could see the top of Wrigley Field. There was a big sign that said CHICAGO CUBS. Lola leaned over to look too.

"He's gone," she whispered to Ben.

Ben looked to the seat where they'd seen the ghost. Sure enough, he was nowhere to be found. As the L slowed and came to a stop beneath the platform's metal canopy, the four of them got up.

"Addison Station," the warbled voice announced on the loudspeaker.

Grandma and Grandpa led them to the door, but Ben kept walking, toward the front of the train car.

"Ben!" Grandma called.

He reached the front and looked down at the seat where he'd seen the kid peeking at him. The seat was empty, save for a half-full plastic water bottle. The boy was nowhere to be found.

Hide-and-seek again, Ben thought. *But what do you want from me?*

———

Ben, Lola, and their grandparents walked down the steps of Addison Station to the street level. After rounding the block and heading down West Addison Street, Ben could see the stadium in all of its glory.

The exterior of Wrigley Field was cool to see, but Ben was distracted. *How could the ghost follow us so far from the apartment? Aren't ghosts supposed to haunt one place?*

"What do you think, kids?" Grandpa asked, motioning to the stadium.

Ben took it all in. The green metal, the massive Cubs sign, the advertising above the entrance to the bleachers. He wasn't a huge fan of baseball, but even he could appreciate how special and sacred Wrigley Field was for fans.

And that was just the outside.

Since they had time before the game started, they

walked around to the other end of the stadium so that Grandpa could show Ben and Lola the world-famous "red sign." The sign proudly proclaimed:

WRIGLEY FIELD

HOME OF CHICAGO CUBS

Below that was a digital display that read:

CUBS VS YANKEES – TODAY 1:20

"We should get a picture," Grandma decided. "With all of us in it. Don't you think? We can send it to your mom and dad back home."

While Grandma and Lola looked for someone to take their picture, Ben looked around for the elusive ghost. If he was trying to play hide-and-seek with him again, he was sure the child wasn't too far away.

"Are you out here?" Ben whispered. With the traffic and crowds filing into the stadium, there was no way anyone could hear him.

He didn't hear a response.

"Ben!" Grandpa called. "Get over here, buddy!"

A man in a Cub's #9 jersey was holding Lola's camera phone horizontally, waiting with a patient smile for Ben to join the photo. As Ben stood next to his sister and in front of his grandparents, the man seemed to concentrate on the screen.

"Okay," he said. "One more."

The man handed the phone to Lola and waited a moment to make sure everyone liked his work. Grandma glanced at the photo for a moment and nodded.

"Thank you very much," she said.

"No problem," the man said. "Enjoy the game!"

As they moved toward the crowd, Ben couldn't help but feel like someone was watching him. He looked through the sea of fans, many of them decked out in various Cubs T-shirts and hats, but he couldn't see the faded face of the ghost boy.

Grandpa handed him his ticket and then another.

"Lola's got her face buried in that phone again," Grandpa said. "Can you take her ticket too?"

Ben turned to scold his sister for being "addicted" to her phone, only to see her face looked pale and almost frozen in surprise. She was staring at the screen like it had some sort of hypnotic power over her. Based on how often she watched videos on it, Ben supposed it did.

"Hey," Ben said, waving the ticket under her face. "Pay attention."

Lola didn't flinch or blink for a moment.

"Look," she whispered, and tilted the phone so Ben could see.

Ben looked at the photo. It was the four of them outside the stadium, taken not even two minutes ago. They were all smiling and looked like they were having a great day in the Windy City.

"It looks good," Ben said. "Send it to Mom and Da—"

"No," Lola blurted, interrupting him. "Look closer."

Ben looked at the picture again. Standing off to the side and looking completely out of place was a figure that time and again over the weekend had made his heart beat a little quicker.

A haunted and hollow-looking little boy stood on the left side of the photo, almost out of frame. He looked back at Ben from the image with his empty eyes and emotionless mouth.

A stranger on the street had captured an image of the ghost.

CHAPTER 9

PLAY BALL

Ben shuffled behind his grandparents, feeling like he was in a trance. It was one thing to see the strange kid with your own eyes and wonder if you were just seeing things. Seeing the image locked into a photo was something else entirely.

Now we have proof, he thought.

He barely remembered showing his ticket to the lady at the gate and realized he had to snap out of it. Coming to Wrigley Field to see a Cubs game was really important to his grandparents. It was especially important to them that he and Lola were there.

Ben leaned over to his sister as they worked their way through the crowd, looking for their seats.

"We have to keep our focus on the game," Ben whispered. "It means a lot to Grandpa."

"Yeah, I know," Lola said. "But it's going to be hard. I just really want to figure out what the deal is with this ghost."

Ben shrugged. "Not sure there's much we can do in a

stadium during a baseball game anyway," he reasoned. "Let's just try and enjoy the game."

"Yeah," Lola agreed. "But it's weird to know he's here, isn't it?"

The thought made Ben shudder a little. The ghost was clinging to him somehow, making sure Ben knew he was around.

What if he never leaves me alone? Ben thought. *Can ghosts attach themselves to people . . . forever?*

He remembered they were due to hop on a bus back to Columbus tomorrow. Somehow, some way, Ben knew he had to be rid of the ghost. He just didn't know how.

Grandpa and Grandma had gotten them great seats behind home plate. Ben was impressed by the stadium, with the ivy-covered outfield walls, the open air and view of the city, and the flags depicting retired jersey numbers flying in the wind.

As they watched the game, they ate hot dogs, had some popcorn, and listened to the way the announcers called action on the field. Ben smiled, watching his grandpa cheer as if every single play was destined to get his beloved Cubs into the World Series.

"This could be their year, Lola!" Grandpa said.

He was still clapping long after #13 swatted a double to score another run for the Cubs.

"Didn't they just win not too long ago?" Lola asked.

"2016," Grandma said. "But before that? 1908."

"Oh boy," Lola said. "That was a while ago."

"Never give up hope," Grandpa said. "That's what makes a fan a true fan."

Ben sat back and watched the Cubs rally from two runs behind the Yankees. In the end it didn't matter. The Yankees stayed on top and won, despite the Cubs' best efforts. Even though his team lost, Grandpa was in good spirits as the crowd rose and began to disperse.

"Sorry, Grandpa," Ben said. "I thought they looked pretty good out there."

"It wasn't their day," Grandpa said with a smile. "There's always tomorrow."

"I'm glad we got to see this place," Ben said, and meant it. "Thanks for taking us."

"Of course, Benji," Grandpa said. "Nothing like being in my favorite place with my favorite people."

"Even if the Cubs lost?" Lola asked.

"Even then," Grandma replied as she put her arm around her granddaughter.

As Ben and his family left Wrigley Field, he took

one last look. He didn't like watching baseball much on television, but being in the stands surrounded by dedicated fans made all of the difference.

And for the first time in a while that weekend, Ben didn't think about the ghost.

———————

Five minutes into the train ride back to the apartment, both Grandma and Grandpa were falling asleep. Ben guessed it was the constant hum of the train on the tracks.

Lola eyed their grandparents. "Do we know where our stop is?" she asked.

Ben tried to think of a landmark that would let them know when they'd need to hop off.

"The river," Ben said. "When we see the river, we'll know we're not too far from their apartment."

To be on the safe side, Lola entered their grandparents' address into her phone's map app and hit START. Instantly, a little dot appeared on the red route south.

"Pretty smart," Ben said.

"Oh, I know," Lola said with a smug grin.

The two of them were silent for a moment, listening to the squeak and clatter of the train moving along the tracks. Ben shook his head and sighed.

"I have to figure out why this ghost is following me," he whispered. "We can't have him get on the bus with us to Columbus."

"And he might be right here watching us now," Lola said. "If only we could talk to him somehow."

A shudder ripped through Ben just then.

"I remember something else he said to me," Ben said. "I didn't tell you last night."

"What? What did he say?"

Ben could hear the sad whisper in his head again, just as clear as he'd heard it his first night in Chicago.

"Why haven't they found me," Ben repeated flatly. "That's what he said."

Lola exhaled as if that was more than she cared to hear.

"Yikes," she whispered, and then she was quiet for a moment.

"So, I don't know," Ben said. "Seems kind of weird, right? Is he always playing hide-and-seek?"

Lola shook her head. "Maybe it means more than that," she said. "Is there something online about the *Eastland* disaster?"

Ben pulled his phone out and did a search. There were a number of articles about the tragedy, and one titled WHAT HAPPENED. He scrolled past it, fairly certain he didn't need to read more about the tragedy. They'd gotten the full story on the boat tour.

"Wait a second," Lola said, pointing at Ben's phone. "Open that one up."

Ben opened a webpage that seemed to be a historical society dedicated to documenting information about the tragedy. It showed a black-and-white photo of the Chicago River. Right below it were details about what had happened.

"It's more about the disaster," Ben said, skimming the summary in the middle of the page. "Oh, wait a second."

He scrolled to the bottom of the page, where there were a number of old black-and-white photographs. One showed the *Eastland* out in the water, with people on the upper and lower decks.

Was the kid in the picture somewhere? he wondered, but then realized he probably wasn't. The tour guide from the Chicago River cruise had said the SS *Eastland* never left the dock.

Additional photos showed people gathered for a group photo. It was obvious all of them came from another time. The men and women were smiling.

A caption below let Ben know the people in the picture were from the previous year's picnic and boat trip.

Lola gasped as she looked over his shoulder.

"The accident," she whispered. "What a nightmare."

Ben tapped the next photo, and it showed the *Eastland* capsized. Onlookers watched helplessly from the shore as people in small boats tried to rescue as many of the passengers as they could. There was a large group of people standing on the side of the ship's belly, waiting for rescue and trying to help where they could.

How awful, Ben thought. *Being one of the survivors standing on the capsized ship, knowing there were people below you who couldn't escape or be saved.*

As much as he didn't want to, Ben zoomed in on the photo, trying to see if he could find someone who looked like the boy. He didn't know much about the kid besides his possible initials and age. He didn't even know if the boy had survived the wreck and died of old age, or if he was one of the victims.

"I don't think this is helping," Lola said. "The photos are too old and blurry to tell anything."

Ben wasn't about to give up. At the bottom of the small collection of photos was a picture that made him hold his breath for a moment.

"That's the morgue," Ben said. "It looks kind of like it did in my dream."

"Whoa," Lola said. "How horrible. Imagine that job, having to figure out who everyone was."

"And who was missing," Ben said. "Maybe there were people they never found."

Lola jerked as if someone had goosed her. Ben guessed she didn't like the thought of that.

Just as Ben thought he'd reached all the website had to offer, he noticed a MENU option at the top of the page, nestled up in the right-hand corner. A drop-down menu appeared with a few options. One of them stood out right away.

"Click that link that says THE PEOPLE," Lola said a little louder than necessary.

Ben glanced at his grandparents to make sure they hadn't woken up from their train nap. Their eyes were still closed. He tapped the option to see what was in there.

"Are we close to our stop?" Ben asked.

Lola checked their progress on the map as they slowed to another station. "We've got plenty of time," she said.

The option to pick between PASSENGERS and EASTLAND CREW was displayed.

"Passengers," Ben and Lola said in unison. There was no way a five-year-old kid was part of the SS *Eastland* crew.

The page took a while to open, but when it did, Ben felt a rush of excitement. There was a list of passengers in alphabetical order. Almost every name had a link taking them to more information. Some even linked to a photo of the passenger.

There was a symbol of a star next to each name. A white star meant the passenger survived, a black star meant the passenger perished in the disaster. To make things even easier, it listed the gender and age of each of the passengers.

"Jackpot," Lola said.

Ben realized what they needed to do. Since the letters *R. S.* were on the bottom of the little boat, that meant the owner's last name likely started with the letter *S*.

That is, of course, if the little boat had anything to do with the Eastland *disaster,* Ben reminded himself. Something told him they were on the right track.

After scrolling through the pages, they found the grouping of passengers they were looking for. Ben scrolled through, looking for initials that matched *R. S.*

"Robert Spencer," Ben read aloud.

"No," Lola said, pointing to the name. "Too old. He's thirty-seven."

Ben nodded and kept looking. Another *R. S.* name came by, but it was a girl in her twenties.

"Richard Samuelson," he read aloud, and glanced at the rest of the information. "He was a male, and he was six years old."

"Maybe that's him," Lola said. "Can you click to see if there's a picture?"

Ben nodded, but he noticed something about the entry. There wasn't a star, black or white, next to his name. He discovered that there were a lot of other names listed that way too.

"What does no star mean?" Ben asked. He scrolled to the legend and found that any entry without a star meant the passenger was "unsubstantiated." He wasn't quite sure what that meant.

"Maybe they couldn't prove they were on the ship?" Lola offered.

"Or even worse," Ben said. "Maybe that meant they were never found."

In his head, Ben heard the words the ghost boy had whispered to him a few nights back.

Why haven't they found me?

CHAPTER 10

GOING HOME

"This is him," Ben decided. "It has to be."

Everything in Ben seemed to point to the name, and he almost expected the little boy to whisper to him and tell him that he was right. Ben even glanced up to see if the ghost was watching him from another seat on the train.

He didn't see him anywhere.

Ben clicked on Richard's name, wondering if he'd be able to see a photo of the boy, like some of the other entries had. When he clicked on it, he discovered a page with a photo of a flower and the message, NO PHOTO AVAILABLE AT THIS TIME.

"What?" Lola cried. "No picture?"

Ben shook his head. "Doesn't look like it," he said. "Not all of them took as many pictures of themselves as you do."

Lola elbowed her brother.

"Well, it's true," Ben muttered.

"But what are we going to do?" Lola asked. "We don't know for sure if Richard is our ghost."

Ben sighed. It seemed they were so close, yet so far away. There didn't seem to be any way to prove that Richard Samuelson was the ghost that had been haunting him and his grandparents' apartment.

As he was about to close the search window, he noticed a small line in a blurb below the photo of the flower. It said that any information about the passenger could be shared by clicking a link.

"They're still looking for information about him," Ben said. "I could write them and let them know we think he's been visiting us."

"Seriously?" Lola said. "You think that's a good idea? A ghost we think might be named Richard is hanging around. Please update your website."

Ben thought about that. He might sound a little crazy to whoever got the email. But then he remembered something.

"It would be kind of strange," Ben said, "if we didn't have proof, but we do."

Lola's face lit up. "You little genius," she said. "Let me send you the photo!"

As they closed in on their station, Ben composed a quick note:

Hello, my name is Ben Tajima, and I think one of the victims from the Eastland *disaster has reached out to me. I never believed in ghosts before, but I'm pretty sure I do now. I think his name is Richard Samuelson. I've attached a photo taken of my family just this afternoon before the Cubs game. You can see Richard in the photo too. I don't think he means any harm but just might be a lost soul. Thank you. Ben*

PS: I found an old toy boat near the site of the disaster with the initials R. S. on the bottom. That's how we thought it might be Richard, but we weren't sure.

"That works," Lola said, after reading what her brother had written. "Send it."

Ben attached the photo and sent the message off. He wasn't sure what, if anything, the message would do. A moment later they were at the station. As if by magic, or because they heard their station announced, both of his grandparents woke up.

"We're here," Grandma announced as if she hadn't been sleeping the entire time.

The four of them got up and hopped off the L. As the train rolled out of the station, Ben watched the windows passing by, almost certain that Richard (if that was truly his name) would be watching them from inside one of the cars.

———

"Anything?" Lola asked as they were getting ready for bed that night.

Ben picked up his phone from the edge of the bathroom sink and checked his email again. Nothing. He hadn't heard a thing back from Eastland Disaster Historical Society.

After that, he'd checked his inbox countless times over the course of the evening. Grandpa had even told him to put his phone away at the restaurant where they'd eaten dinner.

He spit out his toothpaste so he could respond.

"Nothing," Ben replied. "I don't think we're going to hear back anytime soon, if at all."

He started to wonder what the people on the receiving end of the email might think. Some kid in Chicago thinks he's seeing a ghost and it might be related to the *Eastland* disaster?

Delete.

As Ben set his phone back down, he swore he could see Richard's image in the corner of his eye. When he turned quickly toward the shower, he didn't see anything. Even so, that cold feeling in the air came over him.

"What?" Lola asked, watching the whole thing. "What happened?"

"I think I just saw him again," Ben said. "Like really quick."

He shivered and saw Lola rubbing her arms too.

"It got cold in here all of a sudden, didn't it?" Ben asked.

Lola nodded.

"That happened when I saw him a few other times," Ben said. "Plus there was kind of a fishy smell in the air. Like the river."

Lola tightened her mouth and raised her eyebrows.

"Maybe he's mad or something," she whispered.

As soon as she was done speaking, the mirror above the sink began to vibrate. It made their reflections in the glass look shaky, almost slightly distorted.

"We don't know what to do," Ben cried, looking around the bathroom. "I'm sorry! We just don't understand what you want!"

The vibrating stopped, but then a bottle of shampoo fell off the side of the bathtub. Then, the bar of soap. The shower curtain itself started to rustle a bit. Lola backed up as if she meant to escape the bathroom. As she did, the door slammed behind her.

"Stop it," Ben shouted, his voice shaky with fear. "You're scaring us!"

And, just like that, Richard's temper tantrum stopped. It was suddenly so quiet a drop of water falling from the faucet sounded loud.

"Are you okay?" Ben asked.

"Yeah," Lola said. "Just shaken up a little."

"Me too," Ben said. "I didn't know what he was going to do. We might be the closest anyone has gotten to finding him, and we're going to leave."

Lola leaned against the bathroom door.

"He can't follow us," Lola said. "I mean, maybe he could. I have no idea. But we'd probably go crazy."

"And all because I picked up that dirty little boat," Ben said quietly.

He remembered finding the thing wedged into the mud on the sidewalk. It had seemed like a cool little trinket until . . .

"I washed it off," Ben said.

"What?" Lola said. "What are you talking about?"

"The boat," Ben said. "The toy one. None of this ghost stuff happened until I washed the dirt off of the toy boat."

"So what does that matter?"

Ben thought for a moment. "Maybe it's like a magic lamp. You know, how Aladdin rubs that dirty lamp and the genie comes out? Maybe when I cleaned it, it released him somehow. Maybe if I put this back in the mud outside—"

"You think that will get rid of Richard?" Lola asked. "Wow, that's—"

Ben threw his arms in the air. "I don't know," he said, shaking his head. "I don't know what else to do!"

Lola walked over to her brother and sat him down on the edge of the tub. She put her arm around him and looked around the room. Ben looked up at her. His eyes were stinging, almost on the verge of tears.

"Maybe there's nothing we can do," Lola said. "But throwing him and the boat away doesn't seem to be the right thing."

"It's awful," Ben admitted. "This little boy was never found and probably never will be if it's been that long. It's not like we can find him in the Chicago River or

anything. I just don't know what to do. What if he's stuck with us forever?"

As Lola opened her mouth to speak, a loud digital *ding* sounded from the edge of the sink.

They looked at each other.

Ben stood up and grabbed his phone. He unlocked it and saw that he had a single new message in his email's inbox. The sender's name was A. Samuelson.

"I got something," Ben said, staring at his phone.

Lola scrambled to his side as he opened up the email. Together, they read the message.

Dear Ben,

Thank you so much for reaching out to the Eastland Disaster Historical Society. They forwarded the message you sent to me, and I wanted to reply as soon as I could.

My name is Amy Samuelson, and I am the great-great-granddaughter of Mary Samuelson, Richard's mother. The Eastland *disaster is a part of our family's history, as a number of my ancestors were lost in the tragedy, including Richard, who would have been my great-uncle.*

When I asked about the Samuelsons that were lost in the accident, the mention of Richard was always the saddest to hear. I was told he was a mischievous kid who liked to play games, especially hide-and-seek. They believe that he was playing his favorite game when the ship capsized. He was hiding, and no one ever found him.

I'll admit, when I first read your email, I was convinced it was a cruel joke. Only when I saw your postscript about the boat did I realize that your claims might actually be true. Attached is a photo from my family's archive. It was taken the morning of the boat cruise, about an hour before they boarded SS Eastland.

I don't know that I believe in ghosts, but if his soul is still lost, he should know his family hasn't forgotten about him. Maybe that will bring some peace to his spirit.

Thank you again for your message. Be well.
Amy Samuelson

Ben tapped the attachment at the bottom of the message. After a few seconds, a grainy black-and-white photo appeared. In it was a family of five. There was a stern-looking man in a sharp dark suit standing beside a woman in a white dress and a fancy hat. In front of them was an older teenaged girl in a bright dress. A boy, a bit younger, stood next to her. Standing in front of all of them was a small boy of about six years old with dark, neatly combed hair. He was holding something in his hand.

"Zoom in," Lola whispered.

Ben zoomed in on the little boy's hand. There, gripped tightly in his fingers, was a small toy boat.

"It's really him," Ben cried. His heart raced, and every vein in his body seemed to tingle.

He lowered the phone and looked over at Lola. His sister had her hand over her mouth in shock. Neither of them could speak for a solid few minutes.

"I know what to do," Ben said finally.

Late the next morning, Ben, Lola, Grandma, and Grandpa made their way to the Race Dog bus station. Before going inside, Ben walked over to a mailbox on the corner. Lola joined him, telling their grandparents they'd be right back. In his hand, he held a small padded yellow envelope addressed to AMY SAMUELSON in Springfield, Missouri.

"You think it'll help?" Lola asked.

"I don't know," Ben replied with a shrug. "But it doesn't belong to us."

He pulled the metal handle, opening the mailbox door. After taking a deep breath, he dropped it in.

After countless hugs from their grandparents, Ben and Lola Tajima boarded the bus and found their seats. They waited as the rest of the passengers climbed on and got into their own seats.

As the bus finally left the station, they waved to their grandparents, who stood outside, their arms around each other. Grandpa even took off his Cubs cap and shook it in the air.

The bus pulled out of the terminal and headed for the city streets. As it rounded the corner, Ben glanced out the window.

There, standing by the mailbox, was a small boy with dark, messy hair, wearing a dark coat. He watched the bus go by, but his dark, empty eyes locked with Ben's. As they passed, the ghost of Richard Samuelson raised a hand in farewell.

Ben gave a little wave back. "Goodbye, Richard," Ben whispered. "Your family has been looking for you."

AUTHOR'S NOTE

Not many people know that hundreds of passengers and crew drowned on the Chicago River in 1915, but it's the most deadly shipwreck in Great Lakes history. The *Eastland* disaster claimed more passenger lives than the *Titanic* or the *Lusitania*, yet I had never even heard of it before I started researching Chicago history.

Entire families died in the shipwreck, which claimed the lives of 844 people. Richard Samuelson wasn't a real passenger, but there were a lot of young victims from the disaster. The Eastland Disaster Historical Society website lists all of the people who were aboard the ship when it tipped over, including the living, dead, and unaccounted for.

When it came to a setting for the story, I didn't want a haunted house. So I based Grandma and Grandpa's apartment on a real building in the heart of Chicago and across the street from where the tragedy occurred. Ghost hunters believe that the age of a place has little to do with whether it's haunted or not. A true haunting has more to do with the history of the surroundings and what might have happened there.

To add to that, a lot of ghost hunters believe that

objects themselves can be haunted. That was the case with Richard's little toy boat. Since it was an item he carried with him a lot, his spirit became attached to it. Many ghost hunters believe that people leave energy behind when they pass away, and some of that energy can stick around and haunt a place—or even a small metal boat!

The site of the *Eastland* disaster is marked on the Chicago River, at the corner of LaSalle and Wacker Drive, with a sign detailing what happened. Businesses and people who live in the area probably have their own ghost sightings to share. So if you visit the Windy City, consider taking a boat tour. You might just pass over the site of the *Eastland* disaster that claimed so many victims . . . many of whom, like Richard, are still waiting to be found.

ABOUT THE AUTHOR

Thomas Kingsley Troupe has been making up stories ever since he was in short pants. As an "adult," he's the author of a whole lot of books for kids. When he's not writing, he enjoys movies, biking, taking naps, and investigating ghosts as a member of the Twin Cities Paranormal Society. Raised in "Nordeast" Minneapolis, he now lives in Woodbury, Minnesota, with his awe-inspiring family.

ABOUT THE ILLUSTRATORS

Maggie Ivy is a freelance illustrator and artist who lives and works in the Ozark area in Arkansas. She found her love for art at an early age and pursued it with passion. She graduated from The Florence Academy of Art in 2010. She loves narrative elements and story-building moments, and seeks to implement them in her own work.

Eszter Szépvölgyi is a graphic designer and illustrator based in Budapest, Hungary.

DISCOVER MORE

HAUNTED STATES
of
AMERICA

BY THOMAS KINGSLEY TROUPE

A CALIFORNIA
GHOST STORY

A COLORADO
GHOST STORY

A FLORIDA
GHOST STORY

THOMAS KINGSLEY TROUPE

SWAMP
of
LOST SOULS

A LOUISIANA
GHOST STORY

THOMAS KINGSLEY TROUPE

GHOSTLY
REUNION

Illustrated by Maggie Ivy

A MINNESOTA
GHOST STORY

THOMAS KINGSLEY TROUPE

PHANTOM
of the
TRACKS

A NEW JERSEY
GHOST STORY

THE DEAD
BELOW

A PENNSYLVANIA
GHOST STORY

THOMAS KINGSLEY TROUPE

BEWARE
the
BELL WITCH

Illustrated by Maggie Ivy

A TENNESSEE
GHOST STORY

THOMAS KINGSLEY TROUPE

SPIRITS
of
THE STORM

Illustrated by Maggie Ivy

A TEXAS
GHOST STORY